NICK BUTTERWORTH

Q Pootle 5

THE GREAT SPACE RACE

WALKER

Pootle 5's best friend, Oopsy, was singing happily.

"Today . . . today, it's today . . . "

"That wouldn't be the Great Space Race, would it, Oopsy?" Pootle chuckled.

"You know it is, Pootle," said Oopsy. "And this year, I'm going to win!"

She ran off towards her spaceship.

"Don't forget to fix that leak on your Booster," Pootle called.

"I will," Oopsy called back. "See you at the starting line!"

roobie came out of his shack, followed by Bud-D the robot, and found all his friends ready for the start of the race: Eddi, Stella, Pootle and Oopsy. Even Stella's majorbird, Ray, was there, and he didn't like racing.

Welcome to this year's Great Space Race!" Groobie said grandly. "Remember, it's twice round Okidoki, left at the Crumbly Moon, a quick whoosh round Planet Dave and back here to the finish line."

You're in charge of the starting flag, Bud-D," Groobie said. He climbed into his own spaceship. "And don't forget to polish the trophy."

"Ready?" said Bud-D.

The spaceships began to rev, noisily.

"Ready!" each one called back.

"Set?" shouted Bud-D.

"Set!" came the replies.

"*GO!*"

With a great roar, they were off, heading into space.

"Heh-heh, I'm in the lead!" Pootle laughed.

"Not for long!" Oopsy called as she whizzed past him.

"Wow! Look at her go!" said Pootle.

Everyone chased after Oopsy as fast as their spaceships would go. Pootle was getting closer and closer...

Splat! Suddenly, Pootle's spaceship was hit by an oily, dirty splodge.

"Oh, no!" said Pootle. "Oopsy's booster! She can't have fixed it." He pressed a button in front of him.

"Pootle to Oopsy. You have a booster leak. You need to stop – right away!"

t seems alright at the moment," Oopsy radioed back. "See you at the finish line!"

"Oopsy, it's not safe ..." Pootle called. But Oopsy wasn't listening.

**B**ANG!

Oopsy's spaceship began to shake, and smoke poured from the leaky booster.

The spaceship spun out of control, heading straight for Crumbly Moon.

"Poooooooooooooootle!" she wailed.

There was a loud crash, and Oopsy disappeared from view.

"Hang on, Oopsy!" yelled Pootle.

As fast as he could, Pootle headed towards Crumbly Moon and a plume of black smoke.

opsy was dazed and confused as Pootle pulled her from the crashed spaceship.

"Where am I?" she said in a small voice.

"On Crumbly Moon," said Pootle. "With a broken booster."

"Ohhh..." Oopsy was so disappointed.

"I thought you were going to fix that booster," said Pootle.

"I was," said Oopsy, "but...

I was so excited about the race, I just...forgot."

The roar of spaceships high overhead made them both look up.

Eddi, Groobie and Stella were still racing as hard as they could.

Oopsy stared back at the ground.

"I'll never win, now." She looked at Pootle. "And neither will you. I'm sorry, Pootle."

**W**e'll see about that."

Pootle ran over to his spaceship.

He disappeared inside and began to rummage

about for something.

A moment later, he reappeared, holding up

the something.

"Just the job!" he said.

"A plaster?" said Oopsy.

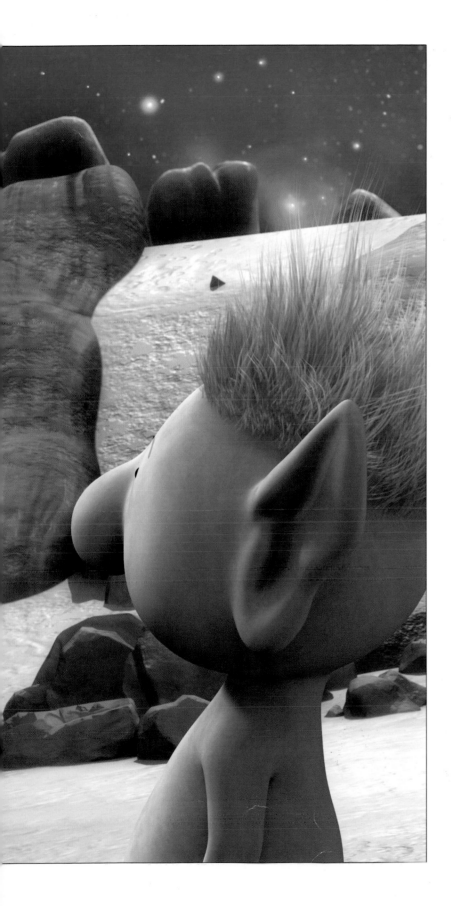

Carefully, Pootle stuck the plaster onto the booster.

"It'll fix the leak until the end of the race."

"But we've got a lot of catching up to do," said Oopsy.

Pootle attached a towrope from his own spaceship onto Oopsy's.

"Then the sooner we get started, the better!"

**G**roobie and Eddi and Stella
whooshed around Planet Dave.
"Ho ho!" he boomed.
"That tickles!"

The three spaceships
raced towards Okidoki.
Groobie and Eddi were neck and neck.
"Groobie's got that winning feeling!" he laughed.
"Faster! Faster!" Eddi urged himself.
"Coming through!" called Stella as she forced
her way between them, into the lead.
"I can see the finish!" said Groobie. "Where's
Bud-D? He should be ready with the flag."

ud-D was ready.

    "They're coming back!" he said excitedly.
"It's Groobie in the lead! No, wait. It's Eddi! Oh!
Make that Stella! Wait..!" Bud-D couldn't believe
his eyes. "It can't be!" he said. But it was...

 Pootle 5's spaceship, now towing Oopsy's, shot past Groobie, Eddi and Stella and was first to cross the finish line.

"Q Pootle 5 is the winner!" cried Bud-D.

ll the spaceships were parked in front of Groobie's shack.

Groobie knocked on the side of Pootle's ship.

"Come on then, Pootle. You're the winner."

"Actually, I'm not."

Pootle was leaning against Oopsy's spaceship.

"Huh?" said everyone in surprise.

"You didn't win?" said Eddi.

"Well then, who did?"

MEEEEEEEEEE!

opsy popped up from the cockpit of Pootle's spaceship with a huge smile on her face.

Pootle laughed. "I was in Oopsy's spaceship," he said. "Oopsy towed *me!*"

Bud-D passed the trophy to Groobie, who coughed importantly.

"Well done, Oopsy," he said as he gave her the trophy. "You are the winner of the Great Space Race!"

Everyone cheered, and Eddi and Stella
hoisted Oopsy up onto their shoulders.
Oopsy looked towards her great friend.
"Oh thank you, Pootle," she said.
Pootle smiled. "Hey," he said.
"That's what friends are for."

Did you spot the space mice in this book?

You have to look carefully. They're very good at hiding!

Text by Nick Butterworth, based on the television series episode *The Great Space Race*, written by Dave Ingham
Images composed by Nick Butterworth and Dan Cripps, produced by series animators Blue Zoo

First published 2014 by Walker Entertainment, an imprint of Walker Books Ltd
87 Vauxhall Walk, London SE11 5HJ

2 4 6 8 10 9 7 5 3 1

© Q Pootle 5 Ltd 2014

This book has been typeset in Gotham Book

Printed in Humen, Dongguan, China

British Library Cataloguing in Publication Data:
a catalogue record for this book is available from the British Library

ISBN 978-1-4063-5901-5

www.walker.co.uk

www.QPOOTLE5.com